Moli det bigibigi

A very special thank you to the Manbulloo family at Kalano for their support for writing this story about Molly.

The Indigenous Literacy Foundation would particularly like to thank Denise Angelo, linguist/literacy consultant from the Australian National University, and Julie Haysom, illustrator, who worked with the Binjari Buk mob to write and illustrate their stories; and HarperCollins*Publishers* Australia Pty Ltd, in particular Eve Tonelli and Hazel Lam, and 1010 Printing International Limited for making the publication of this book possible.

They'd also like to thank the Sanitarium Health and Wellbeing Company for permission to use the illustration of the Weet-Bix packet on page 13.

For supporting the Binjari Buk mob training project, thanks go to Roper Gulf Regional Council, Binjari Community Aboriginal Corporation and the Living Archive of Aboriginal Languages (LAAL).

For supporting Denise Angelo's ongoing research into Kriol, thanks go to: the Australian Research Council (ARC) Centre of Excellence for the Dynamics of Language (CoEDL), the Australian National University and the Australian Government Research Training Program.

A special thank you to Hazel Lam for additional design work on this book.

First published in 2017 by the Indigenous Literacy Foundation
This edition published in 2018, reprinted 2019, 2023

PO Box H38
Austalia Square NSW 1215
www.ilf.org.au

Members of the Binjari Buk mob 2017: Sylvia Birdum, Bernadine Booth, Daniella Carlton, Tasiana Douglas, Marilyn Frith, Rozelle Frith, Halrisha Hodgson, Maureen Hodgson, Sarah Lewis, Karen Manbulloo, Sylvia Maroney, Milly Raymond, Stella Raymond, Natasha Waterloo

Binjari Buk helpers from other years: Christine Anzac, Susan Blutcher, Saffron Booth, Aganita Charlie, Tanya Gallagher, Vivianne Morgan, Noriandra Patrick, Maxine Raymond, Cinetta Ru-unga, Zelda Wurramara

Cataloguing-in-Publication details are available from the National Library of Australia

www.trove.nla.gov.au

ISBN 978 0 6482604 2 4

Editing and design kindly sponsored by HarperCollins*Publishers* Australia Pty Ltd
Printing kindly sponsored by 1010 Printing International Limited, China

Moli det bigibigi

Molly the pig

Karen Manbulloo bin raidim dijan stori
ola Binjari Buk mob 2017 bin drowim ola pitja

Indigenous Literacy Foundation

Dijan iya Moli.

This is Molly.

Im beibiwan bigibigi.

She's a piglet.

Main braja bin faindim
Moli jeya la bush.

My brother found Molly out in the bush.

Imin jidan misalp –
maidi imin git los ...

She was all by herself – perhaps she'd got lost ...

Main braja imin pikimap ...

My brother picked her up ...

en teigimbek la kemp.

and brought her back home.

Ola dog bin beldimbat im wen imin lilwan.

The dogs picked on her when she was little.

BAT imin laigim dagat Wit-Bik.

BUT she liked eating Weet-Bix.

Weet-Bix

En imin gro ...

And she grew ...

En imin gro ...

And she grew ...

En imin gro ...

And she grew ...

En tudei na, im bigiswan bigibigi na!

And today, she is the biggest pig!

Im mo big den dem dog.

She is bigger than those dogs.

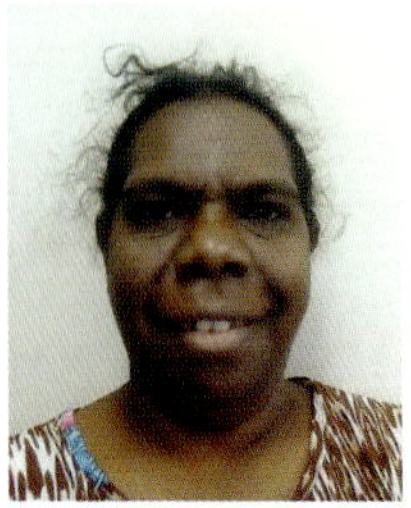

Main neim Karen Manbulloo. Ai bin kam jidan la Binjari 1999 gada main fes beibi. Mela bin kaman iya from Rokhol. En den ai bin aba natha thribala biginini. Wi bin sidan iya fo longtaim na. Ol main bigininimob bigwan na en gadim oun biginini na. Ai laigim gu fishing, hanting, kempinat en shoping. Ai rili laigim sidanbat gada main femlimob ba tok-tok stori, tokabat ba oldendeis stori, en ba wen ai bin lilgel. Ai nomo laigim jidan nathapleis, ai gada stap la Binjari olagijawan.

My name is Karen Manbulloo. I came to live in Binjari in 1999 with my first son. We came here from Rockhole Community. Now I have another three kids. We've all lived here since then. All my kids are now adults and have kids of their own. I like to go fishing, hunting, camping and shopping. I love being surrounded by my kids and my family. We come together to tell stories and talk about the olden days and what life was like when I was little. I wouldn't want to live anywhere else but Binjari.

About Binjari

Binjari is a lovely small Aboriginal community, which is home to about 200 Aboriginal people who mostly speak Kriol. Binjari is located near the Katherine River, about twenty kilometres to the west of the Katherine township in the Northern Territory. It is at the edge of Manbulloo Station, where generations of Aboriginal people worked, including the forebears of many present-day residents. Aboriginal people have developed Binjari as a quiet, safe place for families away from town. In addition to the original Bottom Camp, Binjari has the newer Top Camp area, where most people now live. It has its own office and clinic, and schools and shops are available in nearby Katherine.

About the Indigenous Literacy Foundation

The Indigenous Literacy Foundation (ILF) aims to make a positive difference to the lives of Aboriginal and Torres Strait Islander children by focusing on ways to improve their literacy. We believe that a young child's future educational experiences can be greatly improved through enjoyable and positive engagements with books in the family and community environment at an early age.

Yu gin faindat mo bla dijan Binjari Buk projek iya la websait bla det Indigenous Literacy Foundation mob: www.ilf.org.au

For more project information, please visit the Indigenous Literacy Foundation website: www.ilf.org.au